FIFO 3

There are always three sides to a story...

Aaron Weston

www.facebook.com/aaronwestonauthor

www.instagram.com/aaronwestonauthor

www.tiktok.com@theaaronwhiteshow

DEDICATION

I dedicate this book to my wonderful wife Francesca and to my awesome sons Tyler and Jayden, and to all the fantastic FIFO workers and their families. I hope that you enjoy the book.

DISCLAIMER

This book is a work of fiction. All characters and events in this book are fictitious and any resemblance to real persons, living or dead is purely coincidental.

Bec

Hi reader, my name is Rebecca, but you can call me Bec. Everyone else does. You know how us Aussies are always shortening people's names or putting an 'o' on them like Davo, Jacko or Steveo. Anyway, the author has kindly asked me to share my side of the story. You remember back in FIFO number 1, when I was that horrible wife who cheated on her poor innocent husband. Well, you have heard Mick's side of the story and now you get to hear mine. I'm not saying that my side of the story is 100% exactly what happened. It is just my version of what happened. There are always three sides to a story, yours, theirs, and the truth. We all remember things differently and we all want to put ourselves in a positive light. So, our memories are always more favourable towards ourselves.

Whoa! That's deep. I know right. Just in case you are thinking of closing the book, thinking that this will just be some girl having a winge. I am going to do the hook thing that the author told me to do, to keep you reading. Well, here is the hook, if you do keep reading you will read about threesomes, my experimentation with drugs and a whole lot more. I know you are thinking like what? Well, I don't want to spoil it for you. Just trust me, you will be entertained. If not, that is all good, Aaron's books are not for everyone and that is fine because we all know not everyone has a sense of humour and I guess some people are just soft and easily offended and if that is you. That is all good, just close the book and go and get yourself a mug of warm milk and a hug from someone special. Then you can turn on YouTube and look up Care Bears and you will be back in your safe place where no one can hurt you. Cause apparently sticks and stones can break your bones, but words will hurt you even more.

Alright, now all the soft cocks are gone. This one time when I broke my sex swing and had to use cable ties to fix it... Just joking that did not happen. I buy quality gear with a good warranty. You could put a 200 kg woman in my swing, and it would not faze it.

Anyway, to my story. I guess I should start where Mick started. We first met in Year 8 but did not start dating until we were in Year 10...

I am at Colin's birthday party which is at his dad's property. He has 18 acres which is awesome, as we can crank up the music as loud as we want without anyone cracking the shits.

I am getting tipsy with my bestie Joanne. We had just shot gunned a UDL each and are dancing up a storm. I am keeping an eye out for Luke. Luke is like the hottest guy in our year, and we have hooked up a couple of times at previous parties. I am planning on tonight being the night. I am going to lose my virginity and it is going to be to him.

I have made a pack with Joanne that we will both do it tonight. She chose Johnno to give it up too. Johnno is new to our school, but Joanne and he, have really hit it off. She told me that at the last party they had a little play downstairs. But she was not ready to go any further at that point in time.

"Johnno, you made it," Joanne yells. As she jumps up and gives Johnno a massive hug and kiss. I don't think kiss is the right word, she is basically eating his face off. It doesn't look like he minds too much.

"Hey Johnno, what are you drinking?" I ask.

"Wild Turkey and coke. What about you guys?"

"Passionfruit UDLs."

"Nice. Looks like I have some catching up to do," he replies. Obviously hinting that he is way too sober to be hanging out with a couple of drunk giggling girls. So, he cracks open one of his cans and skulls it.

We hang out talking crap for a while and I feel like the third wheel. Especially when Joanne is sticking her tongue down Johnno's throat every two seconds and rubbing his crotch right in front of me. Stuff this, I'm out. I walk over to another group, who are playing truth or dare.

"Hey Mick, I dare you to ride a sheep," Colin dares Mick.

"Bring it on," Mick replies.

We all follow Colin and Mick over to one of the sheep paddocks.

"Just sneak up behind it and grab the wool behind its head and jump on. Easy. My brothers and I do it all the time," Colin says to Mick who is looking worried. I would be worried too; they are big sheep.

I stand at the fence drinking my last UDL and watch as Mick grabs hold of a sheep. The sheep leaps to action and runs around in circles, trying to throw Mick off. God that guy has some balls, I would have let go and ran away. He just held on like a legend.

Oh shit. The sheep is running straight at us. We all jump back off the fence, just in time.

"Bang."

The sheep and Mick slam headfirst into the fence. Ouch. Everyone bursts out laughing as the sheep staggers off and Mick lays in a heap. It looks so ridiculous. After another thirty seconds of Mick not moving. Colin shits himself.

"Dad, dad," Colin yells and some of the kids climb the fence to help Mick. I am just about to climb the fence too, but out of the corner of my eye I see Luke standing behind one of the sheds and

I instantly forget all about Mick. He will be fine, there are plenty of people going to his aid.

"Hey Luke, there you are."

"Oh shit. Go away Bec."

He looks like he is having a piss, his back is towards me, and his pants are down around his ankles. How funny, you would think at his age he would have learnt to just flop it out without pulling his pants down like a little kid.

"Yeah, piss off Bec. What are you, some kind of pervert or something?" comes a female's voice from in front of him.

WTF. That's Amber's voice. I look down and see her kneeling on the ground in front of him. Oh my God, Oh my God. She was...I got to go. I got to get out of here. I spin around and see Colin's dad loading Mick into the back of his car. So, I just jump in.

"Oh, you're coming too. Okay put your seat belt on," Colin's dad says to me.

"Thanks," Mick says to me, and grabs hold of my hand. Oh, this is random. I look at him, he is a mess, dried blood all over his face and shirt.

"Can you hold this on his head, love?" Colin's dad says as he passes me a towel.

"Okay love," I feel like saying back. Ha ha. Such a dad thing, calling girls, love. I hold the towel against Mick's head to control the bleeding.

We arrive at the emergency department, and they let us go straight through the big double doors into an examination room. I am really impressed by the doctors and nurses. They are very skilful, and I watch as they put the stitches in. It makes me start thinking, maybe I should become a nurse or do something within the medical field when I finish school.

We leave the hospital and over the next couple of days, Mick keeps asking me to hang out with him. He is not as hot as Luke, but he is a nice guy and at least he is not getting head jobs off Amber.

We start dating and it is all good. I study hard and graduate high school top of my class, which gets me accepted into Edith Cowan University to study nursing.

We decide we want to move in together and buy our own home. But no matter how hard Mick works we cannot save up enough for the deposit. I am working at Macca's and studying full time, so I am not bringing much money to the table.

Then one day...

"Hey Bec, Johnno is going to get me a job doing FIFO," Mick says as he walks into my parents' house all excited.

"Cool, is that where you fly up to work and back?"

"Yep, I'll be on the blast crew, blowing stuff up."

"Oh cool. That sounds like a good job for a guy."

"Yeah, and he is driving around a brand new HSV commodore. So, he is obviously raking it in."

"Cool."

"Yeah, really cool. I'll have to be away for three weeks at a time then I will be back home for a week."

"That's ages. I guess it will only be for a year or two and by then I will be a qualified nurse and we will be able to have our own home. Yay! Let's do it."

Fast forward two years and I am a qualified nurse. Yay! Finally, it is so cool. I love my job; it is awesome helping people. Of course, there are crappy bits in the job, like when you have not put the catheter in properly and you end up with somebody else's urine all over you or when an elderly patient soil's himself and as you help him clean himself, he gets an erection. Awkward. But the positives out way the negatives.

Our house is finally built, and we just picked up the keys. Yay! So cool. We stop at a servo on the way to our new house and Mick hops out to refuel the car. The cd player is playing Timmy Trumpet and I want to change it to One Direction. So, I open the glove box to get out the cd case.

"Oh hello, what is this?" I say to myself as a find a ring box and a little note with it.

"Bec, you are the love of my life. I want to be with you forever and have children with you and grow old with you. Will you marry me?" The note says.

OMG, I'm getting married. This is so cool.

"Hey, do you want a drink or anything?" Mick asks before heading in to pay for the fuel.

"No thanks," I play it cool. How exciting I am getting engaged and my dream home all in the same day.

We pull up to our new home. I am happy we paid extra and got the front landscaping included the house next to us did not and it still looks like a construction site.

Mick unlocks the front door.

"Honey we are home," he says, and we both laugh. "Come here. I want to pick you up and carry you over the threshold like they do in the movies."

"Oh, you are such a romantic."

He picks me up and carries me through the doorway. I feel like he is going to fall over and drop me on my ass, so I lean forward and gracefully fall out of his arms and onto my feet. Which is a lot better than face planting it. I look around at the open plan kitchen, dining and lounge. It is quite spacious; I am happy that we took my dad's advice and made the interior bigger than what was originally on the plan. It looked big enough on the plan but, it would have been a shoe box if we had not upgraded it.

"Hey Bec, turn around."

"Yeah, what?" I say as I turn around and there, he is down on one knee with my ring out in front of him like they do in the movies. "Yes, yes, yes. I will marry you."

"I haven't asked you yet."

"Oh, sorry. Well go on then."

"Bec, you are the love of my life. I want to be with you forever and have children with you and grow old with you. Will you marry me?"

"Yes of course," I reply, and he puts the ring on my finger. OMG this is so cool. I cannot wait to tell mum and put it up on Facebook. I call Mum and spend the next half hour telling her everything.

"Hey Bec, are you hungry?"

"Nope. Can you go down on one knee again? I want some photos for Facebook."

I take my ring off and give it back to him and I spend the next half hour working the angles and taking heaps of cool photos.

"Hey Bec, are you hungry?"

"No."

I spend the next half hour adding filters and adjusting the photos to make a romantic collage.

"Hey are you hungry?"

"Oh my God Mick. Why do you keep asking me that?"

"Well, it's 8pm and we haven't eaten since this morning. I have been sitting around here for five hours."

Oh, Wow! Time really gets away from you when you are playing on your phone. It is totally going to be worth it though. I reckon I will get at least three hundred likes and I know for a fact all my girlfriends are going to be so jealous. I post the post and we order some Domino's pizza.

The next day we move all our stuff in, and we christen the house, if you know what I mean. Wink Wink.

We wait a year to get married and we have the wedding at a beautiful winery in Margaret River. It is amazing. I organised the whole thing myself. I wanted Mick to help me, but all his ideas were so stupid like when I asked him what colour flowers he wanted, he said yellow and he wanted to wear a pale blue suit, when the theme of the wedding is all white. Like, Hello. Anyway, I save the wedding by organising white flowers and making him wear a white suit. He also suggested we have a polar bear on the wedding invitations. I was like what is this a Bundy Rum commercial. We chose a white swan, of course.

After the wedding we settle into married life and to be honest it is very routine and boring. Mick would be away at work for three weeks, leaving me to look after the house and I would be working full time. I do try to spend as much time with him as I can on his week off. We go to the movies or out to dinner.

He spends a lot of time in the spare bedroom that we have set up as an office, on his computer, playing games. He stays up very late every night.

I will be trying to sleep and all I can hear is him yelling into his headset about how he is going to shoot someone, or how his team is going to beat the other teams. He plays that Call of Duty which I watched him play it once and it is way too violent for me, I prefer something a bit more chilled like Mario Kart.

To be honest I am getting restless. Maybe I rushed into marrying Mick. I do love him, but he is the only guy I have ever been with, and I feel like I have ripped myself off a bit by not experiencing life more before settling down.

Now let me tell you about Sarah. I know you are like who is Sarah? Well, I will tell you who Sarah is. Sarah is one of the nurses I work with, and she is amazing. During our lunch breaks she tells me the most amazing stories of all the cool things she has done and what she is going to do. Her weekends are always so adventurous. I just want to be her and have her life. Her naughtier stories are mind blowing. The sexual experiences that she has had and still does have sound so bad, I mean bad in a good way.

I will tell you this one story. Sarah invited me to go to a pool party at her friend's place with her and her boyfriend, Tom.

Knock, knock.

Yay! she's here. I open the door.

"Hi, you look nice," Sarah says to me.

I am wearing a see-through cover up and my bikinis and she is wearing something similar. Twinning.

"Thanks, you too," I reply.

"Are you ready to go? Tom is in the car."

"Yep," I say grabbing my bag and locking the door behind me.

"Hi Tom," I say as we approach the car.

"Hey Bec, are you ready for a fun day?"

"Yep, bring it on."

We get to the party, and it isn't the normal let's get pissed vibe like I am used to. It is nice and relaxed. Chilled and classy you can say. Tom introduces me to the hosts Ian and Sara, who are in their early forties, but very fit. They look like they work out regularly. Ian cooks us a gourmet BBQ and Sara offers me a glass of champagne. I feel so classy and mature.

Tom introduces me to another couple Annie and Steve who are about the same age as Tom and Sarah.

"You are so beautiful Rebecca," Annie compliments me, looking me up and down with approval.

"Umm. Thank you. So, are you," I feel like I must return the compliment, I am getting a vibe that she fancies me, even though she has her boyfriend right next to her? It is probably the champagne playing tricks on me. But hey, who does not like a compliment.

"Come for a swim with us," Annie says to me.

"Okay."

So, I take off my cover up and climb into the pool.

"Would you like a refill?" Steve asks.

"Yes please."

I am getting a good champagne buzz on now; I am a bit of a light weight when it comes to drinking. Sarah tells me to just relax and drink as much as I want. She will look after me and Tom will drive us home after, so all good. So that is what I do, I chill out for an hour chatting away and drinking lots of champagne. I am busting for a pee, and I do not want to pee in the pool. What if it comes out yellow and someone sees it? I would just die. It would be my multi vitamin's fault, whenever I have it, my pee turns bright yellow. Anyway, enough about my pee, I cannot believe I just told you that.

I hop out of the pool and dry off. Ian tells me how to get to the toilet within the house. I head inside. It is a nice house, tastefully decorated with photos of Ian's and Sara's adventures. They look like they have travelled all over the world. I walk past one of the bedrooms, its door is half open. I look inside and see Tom having sex with Sara. WTF. Tom sees me and just smiles.

"Come join us Bec," he says, while laying back on the bed with Sara grinding away on top of him.

"Umm," I do not know what to say. I just run away and shut myself in the toilet. I do my pee. WTF was that? I cannot believe Tom would cheat on Sarah. I must tell her; she is my friend.

I leave the toilet and wash my hands in the bathroom. Damn it, I am going to have to go past that bedroom again to get back outside. I set my eyes forward and power walk straight down the hallway, as I pass the room, I tell myself do not look. Even though I told myself not to look I cannot stop myself. I look and there is Sara on all fours taking it from behind. God, they have done more positions in four minutes than I have done in my whole life. Mick and I always just do missionary and it does not last for very long. Like I said, my life is very routine and boring.

I am frozen at the doorway. I tell myself to move forward but my legs do not move. The moans of pleasure coming from Sara are overwhelming me and I am completely jealous of her. I wish it was me in there with Tom. I want to walk into the room and join them. Feel what Sara is feeling. I force myself to walk away. What kind of friend would I be to Sarah if I go in there? What is wrong with me? I am married. Yes, my life with Mick is boring but maybe, if I make some suggestions, he will do those things with me, and I will feel the feelings that Sara is feeling. My body is tingling, and I want to go back into that room. I turn around and no I turn back around and force myself to leave the house and go into the backyard.

Pause break. Whoa, did you feel that reader? That was some Fifty Shades of Grey stuff right there. I have not read the book, but I feel like the vibe would be the same as that. Alright let's see where this journey takes us. Do not worry I am right here with you. Let's do this.

I pick up a bottle of champagne and pour myself a glass and down it. I pour another and walk over to the spa. Sarah and Annie are in there topless with Ian and Steve.

"Come in Bec. It's nice and warm," Sarah says smiling at me.

I look at the food on the table and think I should really eat some of that and sobber up a bit so I can keep my wits about me. Then again, I think I will have a quick spa and then I will eat something.

I hop into the spa next to Sarah, and Ian starts telling us a story about the time he was in Greece. I couldn't contain it any longer and I whisper into Sarah's ear.

"Hey, I have something really important to tell you."

"Yeah, go for it."

"Tom is having sex with Sara in one of the bedrooms inside," I just blurt it out. I do not know how else to say it, so I just say it. I do not know the right way to say your boyfriend is cheating on you. No one prepares you in life to tell a friend that.

"Ha ha. Was that it? Relax he has been with Sara plenty of times. It is no big deal."

"What? Are you serious? Why don't you care?"

"Why would I? We are all friends here. Rebecca, we are all sexual beings. Society just pushes this whole monogamy thing on us. It is so stupid. Look at all those Catholic priests being celibate saying God wants them not to have sex with a woman and where does that get them? They end up taking out their sexual frustrations on kids. Poor little buggers and what about those nuns being celibate, how many stories have you heard about them being mean to the kids in their care. It's because they are all so sexually frustrated. If the priests and the nuns just got it on, then they would leave the kids alone."

She is making sense. She is so smart.

"You told me that you are not happy with your sex life, and it is not your fault. It is due to the closed mindfulness of your husband, and it is not even his fault. He was programmed by society.

Brain washed. I know you want more, and you are allowed to have it. You are a mighty lioness that has been held back by society's chains. But no more, I free you of those chain and give you permission to be your true self."

And with that I feel my bikini top come off and Sarah kiss me deeply and passionately. I try to pull away, but to be honest I do not try very hard. I think I am only pulling away because I feel I am meant too. I give up and lean into the kiss and give myself up to Sarah. Allowing her to have her way with me.

I will let your imagination fill in what happens in that spa. If you want to take a break and just be in the moment, go for it, I totally understand. No judgement here. Wink.

Alright and we are back. I must say that day changed me. I feel more alive now. As if I was blind and now, I can see. I look into the mirror, and I see the lioness that I am.

The following week Mick comes home on break, and I jump his bones. Trying to pull him into as many different positions as I can. Sarah had lent me a book called Kamasutra. Honestly, it is just awkward. Mick just wants to do missionary and I can see he has no real interest in changing it up. He finishes quickly and falls asleep. I lay there unsatisfied and think back to that freeing day in the spa with Sarah, Annie, Ian and Steve, and finish myself off. I lay there for a while with my body tingling and feeling satisfied. I look at Mick, I mean I really look at him. I want him to feel like I do. I wonder if he would be up for it and make the change.

"Hey Mick, wake up," I say, gently shaking him.

"What? What is it?"

"Hey, do you want to have a threesome?"

"What? No? Why do you? No, I love you and I don't want some other girl in bed with us."

"What about another guy?"

"Fuck no. I don't want some other guy having sex with my wife. What is this? Are you joking?"

"Yeah, I am just messing with you. Now that you are awake. What do you want for dinner? I can order some Chinese."

"Yeah, what? Oh good. Umm yeah Chinese sounds good. Thanks."

I put on my knickers and one of Mick's t-shirts and walk out of the room and order the Chinese.

I do not think Mick is the right one to do this journey with me. I call Sarah.

"Hey beautiful girl. How are you?" Sarah answers the phone. Just hearing her voice make me instantly happy and a smile comes across my face.

"Good now I am talking to you."

"Oh, you are so sweet. What are you up too? Do you want to come over?"

Yes, yes, yes. There is nothing else I would want to do more right now than to drive straight over to her place and be with her. I have not turned full blown lesbian. I still like guys. I just love her energy and the way she makes me feel. It's hard to explain.

"I shouldn't, I just ordered Chinese. I told Mick I will have dinner with him."

"I sense you are holding something back. Is there something you want to tell me? You know you can tell me anything."

Wow! She is so in touch with me.

"I just had sex with Mick, and I tried to get him to try some different positions with me, but he just finished early, and I had to finish myself off. Then I asked him if he would be open to a threesome and he almost had a heart attack."

"Rebecca, oh my sweet Rebecca. I am sorry to tell you this, but I do not think Mick is the right one for you. He has such low energy; I can feel that when you talk about him. You are the complete opposite; you are full of white empowering light, and he is holding you back with his dark light. I am not saying he is a bad guy. He is just not the guy for you. For you to come fully into your power, you must release him back into his world. For he is not meant to be in your true world. The world both you and I live in.

Stay with me reader, I know it is going a bit full on, but I did warn you this book is a rollercoaster. Bare with me.

"Yes, you are right Sarah. Is it alright if I chat with you at work about it and you can help guide me?"

"Yes, I am always here for you Rebecca. We will talk at work."

"Thanks Sarah. Bye."

"Bye for now."

I spend the rest of the night with Mick, having dinner and just chilling out. It feels so fake now. Like I am just playing a role, just playing a part in a movie. Just doing my good wife role, holding my true identity inside. I can feel it within, just wanting to come out.

I catch up with Sarah at work and we work out a plan together of how to exit my old life and come into my new one. Mick is now back at work for his three weeks and during this time I am free to be me, the real me, and it is invigorating. I feel reborn. Sarah is right, Mick has been holding me back. I spend most of my spare time over at Sarah's and I just experience life. I take part in a threesome, a foursome, I try role playing, sex toys and I even try bondage.

I invite two of Tom's friends, Dwayne and Phil over to my place for a bit of fun. It is great, we have a couple of drinks to loosen ourselves up and Dwayne even puts a porno on the big screen TV in my bedroom. It has surround sound and that gives the porno a more realistic feel. There is so much good, freeing sexual energy in the air. I have both guys in me and I am on the brink of climaxing when...

"What the hell?"

I turn my head to see Mick standing in the doorway holding a bunch of roses. I instantly feel sick. That poor guy. I do not love him anymore, but still I do not want to hurt him, and I can see the hurt in his eyes.

His eyes change from hurt to anger and he leaps at the guys throwing punches and clawing at them. Dwayne and Phil defend themselves and throw punches and kicks back at Mick.

They start hurting him.

"Stop, stop. Please stop you are hurting him," I yell.

They stop. Mick is laying in a heap on the ground.

"Please go," I say to the guys.

Both guys pick up their clothes and Dwayne gives me a kiss on the cheek.

"I will call you later, to check on you. Hopefully you would have sorted this loser out by then."

"Just go Dwayne."

And with that he and Phil leave the room. I look at Mick, all beaten up on the floor and I burst out crying.

"What are you even doing here?" I ask while at the same time putting my knickers and a t-shirt on.

"My roster changed, and I wanted to surprise you."

"Hey Bec," Dwanye comes back into the room.

"Piss off," Mick says from the floor.

"I would go if this idiot hadn't parked behind me. Blocking me in."

"Oh, okay. Where are your keys Mick?" I ask.

Mick lunges at Dwayne, but Dwayne just pushes him away easily, due to Mick already being badly beaten.

"Stay down idiot or I will beat your ass again."

"Leave him alone," I say as I reach into Micks boardshorts pocket and grab his keys. "I'll be right back," I assure him.

I go out the front to move the car.

"So, do you want to finish this off tonight? Phil is keen," Dwayne asks me.

"No, sorry. Not tonight. I must sort Mick out. I will give you a call during the week." We give each other a quick kiss. Alright back inside I go.

"Does anything hurt?" I ask Mick as I start checking him over for broken bones or any other injuries. His body starts shaking, and he starts to cry. He is going into shock.

"You are just going into shock Mick. Everything will be okay. Just keep breathing and I will be back in a sec. I am going to call an ambulance for you."

I walk into the kitchen and grab my phone off the bench. 000. I order an ambulance and head back into the bedroom. I notice the porno is still playing on the TV and the woman on the screen is climaxing. Lucky girl, that could have been me if Mick had not barged in. I turn it off and face Mick.

"So, what are you doing here?"

"I told you, my roster changed, and I wanted to surprise you," he answers before coughing up blood.

"Actually, on second thoughts, don't talk."

A couple of minutes pass and then I hear a knock on the door.

"Hello, ambulance."

"Yes, in the bedroom," I call back.

They come into the room, and I introduce myself as a nurse and tell them what happened. I recognise one of the paramedics. He works out of Mandurah, Peel Hospital sometimes, Brandon, I think it is, he is hot. I look at his name badge, yep Brandon it is. He gives Mick the green whistle to suck on for the pain.

"Relax Mick, we are going to lift you onto the stretcher and take you to hospital. Everything will be alright," Brandon says. "Do you want to ride in the back of the ambulance with him?"

"No thanks," I answer. I watch his eyes as they go down to my breasts and to my legs. That is when I remember I am not wearing a bar and I don't have pants on only my knickers. My cheeks go bright red, and I quickly throw on a jumper and some shorts. I watch as they load Mick into the ambulance.

"Are you taking him to Peel or Rockingham Hospital?" I ask Brandon.

"Peel," Brandon answers.

"Thanks."

I am in no rush to go to the hospital on my day off. And to be honest I have to prepare myself to break it off with Mick I cannot keep living this lie any longer. I pick up my phone and call Sarah.

"Hey Beautiful," she answers.

"Hi, are you free? I need a friend."

"Yeah, are you okay?"

"Not really."

"I'll be over in twenty."

"K, see you soon."

I have a quick shower and clean up a bit.

Knock knock.

"Thank god you are here," I say to Sarah as I open the door. We give each other a massive hug and I tell her everything that had just happened.

"See, I told you," Sarah says. "You have such a fantastic future ahead of you, but before you can become the lioness you were born to be, you must cleanse yourself of all that negative energy in your life and as I have told you that negative energy is Mick."

"I know, you are so right. You are always right. What would I do without you?"

"You will never have to find out," with that she kisses me, and we make love.

After another shower I call Mick's brother to give him a heads up. Sarah drives me to the hospital, and I see Brandon and his partner again. I have a quick chat with them, I think I will make a play for Brandon in the future, I feel he has good sexual energy. Sarah has really woken me up to myself. I walk past two police officers who are coming out of Mick's room.

"How are you feeling?" I ask.

"Yeah great, I have bruised ribs thanks to your two boyfriends."

"It's your fault. You shouldn't have tried to fight them."

"You shouldn't have been having sex with them."

"Don't yell at me. You shouldn't have been there; you should have been at work."

"What, so this is my fault is it?"

"Well, it's not mine."

"Are you serious? What should I have done? Just walked in and asked the two random guys nicely. Hey, excuse me, if it is not too much trouble, can you please stop having sexual intercourse with my wife and leave my house. Only if that is okay with you. I do not want to inconvenience you too much."

"No need to be a smart arse about it."

Just then a grumpy old nurse pops her head around the door.

"Excuse me; can you two keep it down? There are other people in this hospital, and they don't need to listen to you two carrying on."

"Sorry. We will keep it down," I say. There is an awkward silence for a bit. "I'm leaving you Mick. I have not been happy for a long time."

"What? This is the first time I am hearing about this."

"Listen to me. I've called your brother and you can stay at his place for the week before you go back to work."

"You did what?"

"He will be here soon to pick you up."

"Is this because I said no to a threesome? I didn't want it to ruin our relationship, and I thought you said you were joking about that."

"Do you want to go there? I didn't want to bring this up but if that is what you want," I take a breath and carry on, "when we have sex, it is so boring and routine I find myself faking an orgasm to make it hurry up and end. You do know there are more positions than just missionary, don't you?"

"Oh my God, when did you turn into such a bitch? You are not the Bec I know, who are you?"

"Well, you would know me if you weren't so busy playing those stupid computer games all the time. Who are you playing with anyway? What grown-up stays up until two in the morning playing these dumb games? Oh my god. Grow up."

"Bitch."

"Anyway, regarding the house, I have had it appraised, and you can either buy me out, or I can buy you out. Alternatively, we can sell it. We should end up with five to ten thousand each, after fees."

"Oh my god. How long have you been planning this, and don't you want to at least try to work it out?"

"I have tried, and I am tired of trying. I must do me now. I am allowing myself to be happy. I am finally permitting myself to be happy."

"What the hell are you going on about?"

"I have been seeing someone Mick."

"No shit. Two someones I would say."

"No not them, they are just a bit of fun."

"Wow! Great, I got beaten up just for a bit of fun."

"No, you got beaten up because you were trying to be a hero."

"Piss off."

"Anyway, I have been seeing a lady."

"What? So, you are a lesbian as well?"

"No, but if I want to be one, that would be my choice and mine to make alone."

"What?"

"I am trying to tell you; I have been seeing a lady. She is a life coach, and she told me you are holding me back. I have a fantastic future ahead of me, but before I can become the lioness I was born to be, I must cleanse myself of all the negative energy in my life. Mick, you are that negative energy."

There is a pause in the conversation as he locks eyes with me and just stares at me like I am an alien.

There is a bit more silence and then a knock on the door. It is his brother Shane.

"Hey Bec. Hey mate, are you ready to go?" he asks.

Mick stares at me again.

"Oi Mick, are we going? I have parked in a loading zone and if we get a ticket because you want to be a weirdo, staring into Bec's eyes. You are paying for it."

"Yeah, stuff it. Let's go."

"See ya Bec."

"Bye Shane, Bye Mick."

I leave the room and join Sarah in her car. I tell her everything.

"I am so proud of you. How do you feel?"

I think for a sec.

"I feel lighter. Like a big weight that I had not realised I was carry has been taken away. I feel like I am floating."

"Wonderful and I must say your aura is brighter too. You can stay at mine and Tom's tonight if you want."

"Yeah, that would be great. Thanks."

Next week I email Mick the divorce paperwork for him to sign. I learn you must be separated for twelve months before your divorce can be finalised, but at least I have started the process. I put the house on the market, and it sells quickly. A month later, I book myself a trip around the world and Sarah tells me heaps of great places to go.

Two years later and I am back in Australia. Wow! What an adventure I have had. I am a totally different Rebecca to the one you met at the start of this story. I have been opened up spiritually and sexually. I tried ayahuasca in the Amazon under the direction of a shaman. Learnt breathing techniques from Wim Hof in the Netherlands. I visited the monks in Thailand. I had group sex with

Guru WatWat in India. So many life experiences that I would never have had if I had not freed myself of my past life.

This is where I leave you for now. I hope you enjoyed my story. Remember there are always three sides to a story: yours, theirs and the truth. We cannot trust our memories of past events, as over time our memories change. Anyway, enjoy the rest of the book. Namaste.

Jarrod

Hi guys, I'm Jarrod, and I'm a FIFO worker. I have been doing FIFO for seven years now and yeah, what do you want to know? (Awkward silence). Oh, umm, okay sorry, the author just told me this is not a two-way conversation. Basically, I just tell you my story and you sit there relaxing and enjoy it. Wow! You have it easy. You relax while I do all the hard work, oh well, I guess you did pay for the book. Okay, I will get into it then and tell you, my story.

Well compared to some, I guess it is pretty fucked up and compared to others it is rather good. How you feel about something in life depends on what you are comparing it too.

I started FIFO at the age of 18 years old, after a mate's dad got me a job up where he was working. I started as a hosey in the mill, just hosing down the walkways, under the fixed machines and the conveyor belts. Basically, anywhere the dirt piles up. It was a dirty job and on cold nights playing with water sucked big time, you would freeze to death, well not literally but it was fucken cold. But all good things must come to an end and after six months I got transferred to the crusher area, where I learnt the rock breaker and loaders. After a year there, I got trained up of the dump trucks and have been on them ever since. It is a great job, just cruise around and get a load of dirt from here and drop it off over there. You sit in the air con all day away from the flies. If you get some stand-by you can even have a sleep in the truck. Living the dream.

Life is pretty routine in this industry. Eat, work, drink alcohol, jerk off if you don't have a campy, sleep, repeat. When I started mining, I was doing four weeks on, one week off and it is amazing how quickly everything changes in the real world, one minute there is an old building down the road and after a couple of swings you go back and there is a new

Dome café and a Kmart in its place. Also, one minute your mate back home is dating some chick and at the end of your swing he is with some other bird.

The good thing about the longer swings is that you save a lot of money, this is because you have nothing to spend your money on while you are on site. I spend most of my spare cash on travelling and I donate to an orphanage in Thailand, and to a school in Cambodia. I bet you did not expect me to say that did you?

Well, I have a real soft spot for these kids. They did not ask to be born into poverty, with some being sold off to foreigners, or their parents are tricked into giving them away with the promise that they will be given a better future. Lots of these kids end up being used for prostitution and even body parts.

Body parts you say. Yes, where do you think people get a heart or a kidney from when they cannot get one legally and they are sick of being on dialysis.

They get introduced to someone that can help, for a certain price and because they are so fixated on getting better, they don't ask where it comes from and if they do ask, they allow themselves to believe the obviously made-up story they are told.

So, how did I develop this soft spot? And what do I mean when I said I had a fucked-up story compared to some? I believe the events we go through in life shape us either positively or negatively depending on who we are and our mindset. I heard a good story once that explains it well.

"There were two sons, who grew up with the same alcoholic father. One son grew up to be an alcoholic and when asked why? He answered it was because my father was an alcoholic. The second son grew up and had never touched a drop of alcohol in his life and when asked why?

He answered it was because my father was an alcoholic.

Boom! Well strap yourself in reader and see why I turned out the way I did.

When I finished high school, I did not know what I wanted to do with myself, career wise. So, I decided to have a gap year. After three months of sleeping in and watching TV all day, my dad came to me and told me his brother, who lived in Thailand has offered to pay for a plane ticket for me to go to Thailand and he will show me around. I thought great, why not?

I arrive in Thailand, and it is cool. Well, the temperature is not cool, it is humid. Over the next couple of days Uncle Jeff shows me around the touristy spots and takes me off the beaten track to some of the villages. I do not know Uncle Jeff that well. He moved over to Thailand when I was five years old after divorcing from my Aunt Tina.

Uncle Jeff had bought into a bar just off one of the main drags. The owners were him, a Thai guy, an Irish guy and a Pommie bloke. It sounds like a bad joke. An Aussie, a Thai, an Irish and a Pom walk into a bar. Ha ha.

Anyway, each night, we go to his bar and have dinner there and I hang out with some of the local kids that hang around the bar. The kids range from eight years old to about twelve years old, both boys and girls. I notice some of the patron's chat to the Pommie guy, hand him some money and walk out with one of the kids. I ask Uncle Jeff what the go is with it and he says the patrons use the kids to help them pick up the local Thai ladies or just to translate for them. Makes sense, I guess.

On the last night of my holiday, Uncle Jeff and I are at his bar, and he puts a shot glass in front of me filled with alcohol. I had never done shots before. The only alcohol I have had were some cans of Emu Bitter at a high school party.

"Thanks," I say as I knock it back like the cool people do in the movies. Except I am not in a movie and the alcohol burns my throat and I look like the opposite of cool, gasping for air. "What was that?" I ask between gasps.

"Ha ha. That's tequila. It will put hairs on your chest and on your balls. Here, have another."

He pours me another and another. I do not really want to do it; I feel sick and lightheaded. But I do not want to look like a pussy. So, I do as I am told.

"Have you been with a woman?" Uncle Jeff asks.

"Yeah, yeah of course. Heaps," I slur.

"You're full of shit. Ha ha."

I am lying. I had kissed a girl but that was about it.

"Come with me I have a surprise for you. But first, one more for the road."

I take another shot and as I get up, I fall off my seat. He helps me up and I follow him out to his car, and we go back to his townhouse.

I stumble through the door and the Pommie guy is there, he just smiles at me as he walks past and out the front door to have a smoke. Uncle Jeff walks me up to my bedroom and there sitting on the bed is an attractive Thai girl around my age or maybe a couple years older. I can't really tell in my drunk state.

"Have fun," Uncle Jeff says as he leaves the room. Closing the door behind him.

The Thai girl takes off her top and kisses me. Her perky breasts look amazing. She then goes down on me. It feels amazing and I tell her that again and again and again. What can I say it is my first time and I am very drunk, I am about to blow my load, but she stops just before I do.

"You want sex?" she asks in her Thai accent.

"Yes please," I reply eagerly.

She stands up and takes off her knickers and out flops her, her dick. WTF and it is bigger than mine.

"What the fuck?" I yell. I jump up and run headfirst into the door trying to escape. Bang! I fall to the floor disorientated and as I stand up, I spew all over myself. Uncle Jeff and the Pom open the door and come into the room.

"That's enough. Thanks," he says to the Thai girl boy, lady boy and she just nods her head and leaves the room with the Pom.

"You alright?" Uncle Jeff asks.

"Not really. That was a guy."

"I bet the head was great though."

"Are you serious?"

"Don't worry about it. Get some sleep. But first have a shower and wash that spew off."

I walk, well more like stagger into the shower, I can barely stand up. My head is spinning. I will never drink Tequila again. I dry myself off and lay on my bed. Sleep, sleep? How can I sleep after what had just happened, plus the room will not stop spinning and I am feeling very dizzy.

My mind starts thinking up stupid shit. Like, am I gay now that I got sucked off by a guy? No, how can I be I thought it was a girl and when I found out, I did not go through with it. She had awesome tits though, what? I cannot think that. She is still a he. At least I did not cum. I cannot believe my first head job was from a guy. She was hot though. WTF, stop thinking like that. I eventually pass out.

I wake up to the sound of my bedroom door opening.

"Good morning sleepy head. How are you feeling?" asks Uncle Jeff.

"Like a dog took a shit in my mouth."

"Ha ha. That's the funniest thing you have said all week. Anyway, get dressed I'll take you out for some breakfast before I drop you off at the airport."

"Okay."

I do not want to talk about what had happened last night and thankfully he does not bring it up. I just want to forget all about it and pretend it never happened. The breakfast helps a little and I managed to sleep the whole plane trip back to Australia.

I get back home and start unpacking my suitcase. That is when I see a yellow envelop with something hard inside it. I turn it over and read.

Hi Jarrod, do not open this envelop I have a friend named Tom who will pick it up on Thursday at 1pm. Do not tell your parents. Otherwise, something bad will happen. Email me straight away after you read this.

I email Uncle Jeff.

Hi Uncle Jeff, what is the go with this envelope? What is in it? and what is the bad thing that will happen if I tell my dad?

I get an email back straight away with an attachment.

Hi Jarrod, sorry to get you involved. Just do as you are asked, and everything will be all good. As for the bad thing... Open the attachment and have a look. If you do not do as you are asked this will get sent to everyone you know on social media.

I open the attachment, and I watch a video of me getting a head job off the ladyboy and his dick coming out and me running headfirst into the door. I do not want my friends seeing this.

I put the envelope under my bed, and it stays there for the next two days. It is consistently on my mind. What could be in there? the guy is picking it up this afternoon. All I have to do is not touch it until then, but I cannot help myself. I just have to know what all this fuss is over. What could it possibly be? I YouTube how to open a letter undetected and watch as a bloke opens a sealed envelope by using steam. The steam softens the glue enough to open it. So, I take it downstairs to the kitchen and boil the kettle. Using the steam made from the kettle and a knife I gently open the envelope without tearing it.

I stick my hand into the envelope and pull out a portable hard drive. I take the hard drive and the envelope back up to my bedroom. I connect the hard drive to my computer and open it up.

There are heaps of files on the screen labelled with people's names. I click on one of the files labelled Benny and heaps of videos pop up, I open one of the videos to see the face of one of the kids that I had been hanging out with at the bar. What happens next is horrifying. I do not what to repeat it. It traumatises me and the last thing I want to do is traumatise you. Basically, it is child porn. I click on a second one and see it is the same kind of thing. I wish I had never opened that envelope.

I put the hard drive back in the envelope and get a glue stick from my dad's office and glue it shut.

What should I do? Should I call the cops? How bad are the guys that do this stuff? I mean, are they mafia types? Will they kill me and my parents? I think the best thing I can do is just hand it over and forget this stuff ever happened. And that is what I do. I hand the envelope over to Uncle Jeff's mate and bury that stuff deep down inside my head and pretend it never happened.

I email Uncle Jeff and tell him it is done and to never contact me again. He never does try to contact me and a couple of years later I see him and his mates on TV, their bar is getting raided, and they are all arrested. Karma.

That is where my passion for helping kids comes from. I join up with a local church organisation who go over to countries like Cambodia and help their communities. I help in an orphanage and at a local school teaching kids how to speak English, but I feel I am not doing enough, and neither is the church organisation. Not because they do not want to, they just do not have the money to do it. They are relying on donations. That is when I go back to Australia and hit one of my mates up. I know his dad works FIFO and that he earns a lot of money. My mate asks his dad, and his dad sets me up with a job up North with him.

The money I earn from FIFO makes a massive difference over in these countries. Especially as I earn Australian dollars and after it is converted to Thai Baht or Cambodia's Riel it is a lot of money, and labour is cheap over there too. So far, I have helped hundreds of kids learn how to speak English, have access to clean drinking water and a safe place to sleep. Thank God for FIFO.

I take Bob, one of my workmates over to Thailand on our week off.

"Jarrod this is heaven," Bob says.

Poor Bob is not the best-looking bloke, he is 5 foot 4 inches with a massive gut on him. But over in Thailand having a big gut on you means you can afford a lot of food, so basically you are a rich person by their standards. Lots of the bar girls pay him attention and want him to take them back to his hotel room. He buys them drinks and laps up the attention. Since I have been over to Thailand so many times before I know all the tricks these bar girls play. They get a commission off the drinks the patrons buy them. So, when Bob buys them expensive cocktails, they will just get a non-alcoholic drink in a glass, but Bob will get charged the price of the cocktail. This way the girl gets maximum commission, and they keep their wits about them, by not getting drunk. Once the girl talks the patron into taking her back to their hotel room the patron pays a bar fine to release the girl from the bar, this is because the bar will lose money from the girl leaving as she is not there to talk patrons into drinking more and buying them drinks.

The girl barters with the patron on the price of her services for either a short time being an hour or two up to a long time which is normally staying the night and leaving in the morning.

If the girl is smart enough, she can talk a lonely guy into paying for her services for the entire time the guy is on holiday and even go on tours with him to keep him company. The smart ones gets the guy to book their tours through the girl's friend for a "good price" which she will get a commission from. 99% of these girls are not sex slaves or forced to do it, as some people may think. They come from neighbouring villages in lure of the easy money and a fun time.

Some of the girls can talk multiple guys into sending her money over each month to stop her from having to sell her body and to act as if she is the guy's girlfriend. Lots of these guys believe the girl is being faithful and that she is his girlfriend. Not knowing that she has multiple guys doing the same thing and at the same time meeting new clients at the bar. I guess you cannot blame the girls for trying to earn as much as they can in the smallest time frame that they can. These girls do have a shelf life, once they hit an older age, the foreigners will look more towards the younger, more attractive ones for their entertainment.

After the trip I find out that Bob did get suckered into one of these girlfriend experiences. He met a bar girl named Joy who is less than half his age and weight. I tell him he is being suckered, but he does not want to hear about it. He is in love. So, I let it be. Apparently, he is sending her over a couple of hundred dollars each month and maybe that is not too bad considering Joy is way out of his league if she was over here is Australia. A girl who looks like her would not look twice at him over here. So, whatever, good luck to him. Maybe they will get married and she will have a couple of kids to him, obtain her Australian citizenship and then leave him and get paid child support for the next

18 years. That exact scenario has happened more than a couple of times to guys doing FIFO. I must be fair, there have been a lot of these marriages that do work out.

We will leave Thailand talk and head to work talk. I land in Port Hedland, and I make my way over to the baggage carousel and I sneak up on Mick, who is one of the other dump truck operators.

"Hey Mick," I say.

"G'day Tim. How was your break?" he asks.

"Yeah, not bad. Watched some movies, went wake boarding with some mates. I got pissed. Yeah, pretty standard. Next break will be better. I am off to Thailand. Too bad you're married, or you could come over with me."

"Yeah, too bad."

Oh, I forgot to tell you my nick name is Thailand Tim. Everyone thinks I am one of those dodgy young guys hitting up all the cheap Thai girls every break, but you know why I am really going over there. I used to correct people and tell them what I am doing over there but I got too many people just smiling and agreeing or not really giving a shit. So, I just gave up and let them think what they want. I also don't mind taking over the odd work mate so they can experience Thailand and Cambodia and if all they want to do is the touristy stuff and the cheap girls. That is fine I still enjoy myself and it is nice seeing other people have fun.

Back to the story.

"She looks alright. What do you reckon?" I ask Mick, while looking at a tall brunette. We head over and have a quick chat. Her name is Jackie, and it looks like we will be working together. Lucky me.

For the next week I flirt hard with Jackie, giving her the odd wink, smile and the old lock eyes with them and be the first to look away trick. You know the standard flirting techniques to let them know that you are keen if they are keen.

It is finally shift change and game on. If Jackie plays her cards right, she might just get to meet the J Rod, get it because my name is Jarrod, and it is my rod. Ha ha. Don't worry it is never funny once you have to explain it.

Anyway, we are having a great time drinking and playing doubles at pool, me and Jackie verses Mick and Sofia. Jackie is surprisingly good at pool, she is a bit of a Tom Boy which is good, it means when we start dating, we can do fun guy stuff like wake boarding, instead of boring girly stuff like romantic dinners. Boring.

The bell rings for last drinks and I tell Mick to go and get some lemons and a saltshaker, as I have a bottle of Tequila in my room. I know I told you I would never touch Tequila again but one of my mates bought it for me three months ago for my birthday, so I just brought it up to work and left it in my room. I take the girls back to my donga and crank up some Metallica.

"Oi Tim, you better turn that down," Mick says as he rocks up to my room.

"What did you say? I can't hear you over the music."

"I said you better turn it down before we get in trouble."

"Yeah alright, alright. I will turn it down. You get the lemon and salt."

"Yep."

"Sweet," with that I go into my room and turn down the music. I quickly wash out a couple of coffee mugs and grab the Tequila.

"So where are the lemon slices?" I ask.

"Lemon slices? You asked for lemons."

"No, I did not. I asked for a saltshaker and lemon slices."

"Whatever. Anyway, have you got a knife or something?"

"No. I have a pen. We could cut the lemons up using the pen or what about a toothbrush? That would work."

"Oh my god. You two are idiots. We can peel the lemons. They are already in individual pieces under the peel," Sofia says shaking her head.

"Oh yeah. I knew that. I was joking about the pen and toothbrush," I laugh. I must admit I am pretty pissed. I did not eat any dinner and I got straight on the bourbons after work.

So, we all peel a lemon each and pull them apart into individual pieces. We place them into my work lunch box, and I pour shots of Tequila into the coffee cups. I see Mick examining the cleanliness of my coffee mugs.

"Don't worry. I rinsed the cups out in the shower," I say.

"The shower? Why would you rinse them in the shower and not in the sink?"

"The shower does a better job," I reply. God what a dumb question, every knows that. Just look at how much water comes out of a shower head compared to a tap. Sorry to say I do not think Mick is the sharpest tool in the shed.

"Umm, okay. Fair enough I guess," he replies.

We all take turns of taking a shot of tequila from one of the coffee cups, licking the salt off the back of our hands and then sucking on a piece of lemon. Everyone is becoming extremely drunk, and the volume of our voices increase as we all try to talk over each other as you do when you are drunk. Security comes past and tells us to keep it down. They say if they have to come back again, we will have to call it a night or be reported.

"Hey, hey. I have a funny story for you," Mick says.

"Go on," we all reply.

And he tells us the whole story about his wife Bec cheating on him with two guys. Wow! What a slut. He is up here working his arse off, and she is back home having gang bangs. Luckily, they don't have kids together. That would make the whole thing messy, and you never want kids having to go through that crap.

"Oh, I'm so sorry," both girls say.

"I know how to make you feel better Micky boy. Come to Thailand with me this break," I say.

"Ha ha. Good one. I can't do that."

"Why not?"

"Yeah okay. Why not?"

"Awesome I will get my flight itinerary, and you pull out your phone and credit card."

"What, you want me to book it right now?"

"Yep, otherwise you will chicken out."

I go into my room and find my itinerary. I grab Micks credit card off him and book him a plane ticket. I also upgrade my room to accomdate him.

"Let's celebrate Mick's new life," I say. The girls cheer and we do another round.

I guess that last shot was Micks one too many and he stands up, takes two steps forward, and power spews all over the red dirt in front of my room. I wonder if I will come out in the morning and find a bungarra licking that spew up.

"I think I will call it a night," Mick says.

"Me too," says Sofia, "are you coming Jackie?"

"Na. I think I will stay and have a couple more with Tim."

"Ha ha. Okay have fun," Sofia smiles at Jackie.

I wave to them as they both stumble off towards their rooms. Silly Mick should be going back to Sofia's room. Sofia stands there on the pathway for a sec to see if Mick is going to follow her to her room but he beelines it for his. So, she gives up and keeps on stumbling off to hers.

"I want to do the lemon and salt off your tits," I say to Jackie.

"Only if I can do it off your chest,"

"Deal."

We go into my room and lock the door. Our tongues are down each other's throats, and our hands are ripping off each other's tops.

"Nice," I say as I check out her tits. They are fakies probably a good size C cup. I lay her down and shake some salt onto her nipples, pour some Tequila into her belly button and I put a lemon slice into her mouth. I lick the salt, suck up the Tequila and fish the lemon slice out of her mouth with my tongue and eat it. She rolls me over and does the same. Then I roll her back over onto her back, undo the button and zipper of her short cargo shorts, grab hold of her knickers and shorts and pull them down to knees.

"What the fuck?" I yell in shock. My body twitches all over and I am instantly filled with rage. There in front of me is a dick and it is not mine. I get a flash back to when Uncle Jeff tricked me into getting a head job off that ladyboy. And now I have this thing in front of me again. I feel like punching Jackie right in the face. My hands close into fists and Jackie springs to life, pulling her I mean his knickers and shorts back up and grabbing her I mean his top.

"I thought you knew," she / he yells at me.

"Get the fuck out of here before I smash your fucken head in."

She legs it out of my room and down the pathway pulling her top on as she runs. How dumb am I? How did I not know? I have seen plenty of ladyboys in Thailand and Cambodia. You would think I could spot a ladyboy easily. She had me fooled. I am the fool. How stupid can I be? I throw my fist into the bathroom door, and I do it again and again and again until the door is shattered and barely hanging onto its hinges. I slap myself across the head a couple of times. Stupid, stupid. I sit there for a long time and eventually pass out.

I sleep most of the day and I get up at three in the afternoon. I skull some water and make my way to the gym. I still feel angry at Jackie and angry at myself, so I walk into the gym and spend five to ten minutes hitting and kicking the crap out of the boxing bag. I cannot spend much more time than that, it wears you out. I do not know how boxers and Mauy Thai guys go for so long. I guess they train a lot more than I do. I head back to my room and get ready for work.

I head into the dry mess and grab some dinner. I sit at my usual table and I am happy no one else is here. I just want to be alone.

"Hey Tim, I thought you would be sitting with Jackie," Mick says before sitting down next to me.

"Piss off," I reply angrily.

"Woo, woo. Did I miss something here? You two looked cozy last night. What happened?"

I guess I should calm down. This crap is not Mick's fault.

"Sorry Mick. I don't want to talk about it."

"Wow. Must be serious I have never heard you talk like that before."

"Yeah sorry. Now can we change the subject?"

"Umm. Okay then."

We sit in awkward silence for a bit and just eat our food. I think one of us had better say something, to break this awkwardness, so.

"So, are you excited about the trip?" I ask.

"Trip? What trip?"

"Ha ha. What trip? Our Thailand trip, this break."

"What do you mean? I'm not going to Thailand."

"Yes, you are. You booked your ticket last night."

"Umm, I think I would remember booking a plane ticket."

Wow! I knew he was pissed but not that pissed.

"Check your emails on your phone. You should have received your confirmation and flight itinerary."

Mick pulls out his phone, and sure enough, there is an email from Virgin confirming his flight to Thailand.

"Wow. I guess I am going to Thailand."

"Yep, and it is going to be awesome. We can go and watch the Muay Thai, hire some motorbikes, go parasailing, get massages and you can even get a bar girl if you want."

There is an old saying the best way to get over a girl is to get on top of another girl. I guess girls can use the same saying except make it. The best way to get over a guy is to get under another guy. Boom! Words of wisdom.

"Yeah, sounds cool. What about accommodation?"

"Don't worry about that. I upgraded my room last night to a suite with two double beds."

"Awesome. Boy's trip," we high five each other and laugh. Then we finish our dinner and head to the self-testing machine.

"0.02," I say.

"0.01," Mick says.

"Sweet. We will both be blowing zeros by the time we make it to work."

With peace of mind that we won't blow numbers, we hop onto the bus to go to work. I see the girls sitting in their usual seat. Fuck Jackie.

"Hi ladies," Mick says smiling like an idiot.

"Hi Mick," they both reply.

I just ignore them and keep walking to my seat.

"Hi Tim," Sofia says.

"Oh. Hi Sofia," I reply.

It is a bit hard to ignore Sofia when she is literally saying hi to me. I wonder if she knows what Jackie is. She would have to. I wonder if she is laughing at me. She does not look like she is. Jackie would have told her; girls always talk to each other. But then again Jackie is not a real girl.

I avoid Jackie for the rest of the week, and before I know it, it is that day, what day? Fly out day.

Whoop, whoop! We fly into Perth, and I catch up with some mates and have a relaxing day. I do not dare tell them want happened, most of my mates are in mining and they would just pull the piss out of me. Big time.

The next morning, I meet Mick at the airport, and we fly to Thailand. It takes us seven hours to get there, which is 3 movies and a nap. We arrive at the airport and get our lift to the hotel.

It is your standard Thailand hotel, frangipanis everywhere, pools with swim up bars. It has a very relaxing vibe. We get changed and head down to one of the pools.

"Ahh. This is the life, hey Tim."

"Yep. It sure is."

We relax in the pool, drinking the local beer for about an hour. Then a bell sounds, ding ding.

"Happy hour. Half priced shots," calls out the bartender.

"You keen," I ask Mick.

"Bring it on."

Mick and I go shot for shot for the full happy hour. We are having a great old time and I am flirting away with some Germans. I see George and his girlfriend, and we have a couple of shots with them. George is massive and good to have around. You can play up if you want to and no one would dare mess with you. That being said, I don't act up too much, you do see a lot of Aussies that get too pissed and act like idiots over here and they give us a bad name. George's girlfriend is getting a bit loose. She has a massive bikie skank vibe, but she is cool. She just does not give a shit. She pulls her bikini top off and is swimming around the pool topless until the Thai security guards come up to ask her to put her top back on. It is funny when they see George and start calling for backup. It takes 5 Thai security guards to get her to put her tits away.

"Hey bro, I'm going to take her back to the room and get her some food. We might see you later," George says to me.

"Yeah, too easy."

And off they go. I figure we might as well change the scenery too.

"Come on Mick. Let's get ready and I will show you the nightlife."

"Bring it on," he replies.

We get out of the pool and grab our towels. We are only halfway back to our room. When Mick suddenly throws up in the manicured bushes next to the walkway.

"Yuk. Dad, look at what that man is doing," a little girl says. As her family walks past us. Ha ha. Welcome to Aussie miners on holiday young lady.

After Mick finishes his spew, we walk back to our room, and I make him skull some water and have a shower.

"Feeling better Spewy?" I ask.

"Yep, I think the trick is to eat when you are drinking. The liquid only diet does not seem to work for me. Ha ha," we both laugh.

"Come on Mick I will show you the real Thailand."

"Bring it on."

God, he says bring it on a lot. I wonder if he has watched that Bring It On movie too many times. You know the one with the hot cheerleaders in it. I reckon the dark-haired chick is the hottest of the two main characters.

We rock up to the restaurant and get seated at a table in front of the stage. I have been to this restaurant plenty of times. It is cool watching the Thais do their traditional dances in their traditional get ups and the food is authentic Thai, where the mild is hot, medium is very hot and hot is lava. I piss myself laughing watching Mick try to eat his mild food, burning his mouth with every bite while trying to pretend it is not hot.

"How's your meal?" I ask.

"Yeah awesome. Very flavoursome."

"Is it hot?"

"Na, this is piss weak. I have had way hotter."

"Ha ha. You are full of shit. Do you want me to order you some milk or ice cream to cool your mouth down?"

"That is probably a good idea. Ha ha."

I order us some desert and the ice cream does the trick for young Mick.

"You up for some Muay Thai?" I ask.

"Oh yeah I like kickboxing."

"Well, technically Muay Thai is not kickboxing. Kickboxing is kicks and punches. While Muay Thai has knees and elbows as well."

"Oh, okay. I stand corrected. Yep, sounds good."

"Cool. We will finish these beers and head over."

It is only a ten-minute walk down the road to the Muay Thai ring. But it takes us thirty minutes because Mick keeps stopping to look at the stalls selling the fake Hugo Boss belts, Rolex watches, and Billabong t-shirts. I help him barter down the guy selling the Rolexes.

"How much for this one?" Mick asks the guy.

"6000 baht."

"6000 so that would be around $200 Aussie. God that's good. Yep, I will have that one. Thanks."

"No way will I let you buy that watch for that price," I say. "Let me handle this."

"He will give you a thousand baht," I say to the Rolex guy.

"Ha ha. I would buy it off you for a thousand baht," the Rolex guy replies, "make it two thousand, you are an Australian. You have lots of money."

"No thanks, I will go down the road to another watch guy, he will do it for me for that price," and I start walking off.

"What the fuck? I really wanted that one," Mick says.

"Shut up and watch this."

"Okay, okay. Fifteen hundred baht, no less. Come back. Okay it is a deal," the stall guy says angrily.

"That is fair. Pay the guy Mick."

And there you have it ladies and gentlemen that is how you barter in Thailand.

"Now can we go to the Muay Thai ring?" I ask. "I promise you will have plenty of time to buy all of your fake stuff before we fly home."

"Yeah alright. Thanks for getting me the watch so cheap. The next round is on me," he replies.

He cannot stop looking at the watch and mucking around with the settings. He is like a little kid who found his dick for the first time.

"Stop playing with it or you will break it."

"Yes dad. Ha ha."

We finally make it to the Muay Thai ring. Bang, bang, thud, thud. These guys really go hard. I guess it is their national sport. Muay Thai to the Thai's is like AFL to us Aussies. Go the Eagles. Ha ha, I bet you the reader are thinking about your own footy or rugby team right now.

We find a seat on the benches surrounding the ring and true to Mick's word he orders us a round of beers.

After each fight, the fighters walk around the crowd, and we give them a hundred baht each for watching their match.

The announcer comes into the ring.

"Hello everyone, we need a volunteer from the crowd to fight one of our fighters," the announcer calls out to the crowd. That sounds perfect for Mick. So, I yell out to the announcer.

"Hey, over here."

"Wonderful. We have a volunteer. Please come down."

Mick looks at me surprised.

"Well get up and go down," I say to him.

Now he looks at me very surprised.

"What? You are the idiot that put your hand up."

"Yeah, that was for you. Don't worry; they go soft on the tourists. Think about it, they would not make any money off the tourists if they beat them up. Now, would they?"

"That makes sense. I guess," He stands up, skulls the rest of his beer and makes his way down into the ring. The audience gives him a big cheer.

I cannot wipe the smile from my face I look across the ring and see George, Johnno and their girlfriends, we make eye contact and I give them a wink, to say, watch this, it's going to be good. Ha ha.

Mick turns to the crowd and does a fist pump in the air. The crowd gives him a cheer. I see the announcer talking to Mick and then puts some gloves on him. Game on.

The guy he is versing looks all of twelve years old, but you know how these Asians look younger than what they are. He is probably nineteen or twenty and probably has been fighting since he was two.

The announcer dings the bell.

"Fight," he calls out.

Pow, bang, bang, thud and Mick is on his arse. He had push kicked him in the stomach and then punched him twice in his side. Mick looks like he is going to throw up. Game over for the Mickstar. What is this? He is getting back up ready to go again. Wow! Great stuff Mick, I thought you would have been softer and had a cry and come back to your seat.

The crowd cheers for him and then pow, bang, bang, thud. Mick is back on his arse again. The kid had push kicked him in the stomach again with his right foot, kicked him on his side with his left leg and finished him with a kick to his head with his right leg.

Mick is not moving so I put down my beer and run down there. God, I hope I have not gotten him killed. I do not want that on my conscience.

"Do something," I say to the announcer.

I put Mick in the recovery position like how they trained us in the first aid course we did through work. Making sure his airway is open and he has a pulse. The announcer gets some smelling salts or tiger balm smelling stuff and waves it under his nose.

"Come on buddy wake up," the announcer says not looking too worried. He probably sees this all the time. Mick's opponent has his gloves in the air in the normal victory celebration style.

Mick comes to and stands up.

"He is all good," calls out the announcer. "Who is next?"

There are no more volunteers.

"All good, we have more fighters here ready for your entertainment."

I help Mick back to our seats and the crowd cheers for him. I order us another beer each.

"That was awesome. I cannot believe you had the balls to go in there. I would never have done that," I say, as the waitress hands us our beers.

"What? And I thought you said they go soft on tourists?"

"Oh, yeah, I lied, they go harder. Ha ha," I laugh, "at least you have a good story to tell Sofia."

"Why would she care?"

"Umm. Maybe because she fancies you."

"No way. She is totally out of my league."

"Yeah, I think so too. Jackie told me she does though."

"Speaking of Jackie. What happened between you two?"

"Don't go there, Mick. It will just ruin the good time we are having."

"Okay. I'll drop it."

"Might call it a night. What do you reckon?" I ask.

"Sounds good. I am feeling pretty sore. Thanks to you."

"Don't blame me, you could have said no."

We go outside and wave down a tuk-tuk. As we are getting in George, Johnno and their girlfriends walk up.

"Hey Mick, good on you for giving it a go," Johnno says.

"Ha ha. Thanks, Tim tricked me into it."

"Well at least you have a good story to tell Sofia."

"Ha ha, that is what I said," I agree.

"What? Am I the only one that does not know that Sofia likes me?"

"Well, I don't," George's girlfriend Trace pipes in.

"Ha ha. Yeah, well everyone at work knows. You guys want to come out nightclubbing with us?" George asks.

"Ha ha. No thanks. We had better let our Muay Thai fighter here get some rest. Who knows he might even have a concussion? You guys have fun," I say.

"Ha ha, you too," says George.

With that Mick and I hop into our tuk-tuk and head back to our hotel.

The next morning, I wake up and see Mick is snoring his head off, so I jump in the shower. As I get out, I hear Mick groaning and moving around.

"How are you feeling?" I ask.

"Like crap. I have the sorest head and check out this bruise," he says while lifting up his shirt.

"Well lucky you are in Thailand. You can get almost anything from the chemists here. After breakfast, I will pop down and get you some pain killers."

We go down to the breakfast area, which is overlooking another one of the hotel's swimming pools. There is everything available for breakfast; six different types of freshly squeezed juices, ten kinds of cereal, bacon and eggs, omelettes and the list goes on. This buffet puts the mine site's buffet to shame.

I get some croissants, a coffee and a glass of fresh mango juice. We pick a nice table close to the pool.

"Ahh, besides the bruised side and throbbing headache, this is paradise. Ha ha," Mick says.

"Ha ha. Yep, it sure is."

"I can see why you keep coming back."

I just smile in reply and finish my breakfast.

"I am going to pop down to the chemist now. How strong do you want your painkillers? Slight pain relief or cannot feel your face pain relief?"

"Just normal thanks. I still want to have some fun today and not be totally out of it."

"Yep. No worries. See you soon,"

I walk down the road to the local chemist it is only a five-minute walk. I must remember the shopping list my mates from back home asked me to get them. Pete wanted a packet a Valium and Terry wanted a packet of Viagra. I order those and some painkillers from the pharmacist. No script needed. He does not even bat an eye lid; he is probably used to Aussies coming over and ordering their penis pills and whatever else.

"With the pain killers just take half a pill to start and in four hours take another half. No alcohol," the pharmacist says to me.

"Will do. Thanks."

I get back to the hotel and Mick is chilling in the pool with a beer. So much for the no alcohol. Oh well, I am sure a couple of beers won't hurt.

"Here you go," I say handing him the pills. "I am going to grab a towel."

I go over to the towel station and grab a fresh towel. Time for a beer and a swim.

"Just take half a pill to start off with, and in four hours you can have another half," I tell him.

"What? I just took two."

"Why would you take something, when you don't know what it is?"

"Because you gave it to me."

"Wow! If I jumped off a cliff, would you, do it?"

"No. Oh no. What do you think will happen now?"

"Calm down drama queen. I reckon you will feel really relaxed."

I order a beer and we spend the day relaxing by the pool. Mick passes out for most of it. I order us some lunch from the swim up bar and when I swim back to Mick, he is talking out loud about Minnie Mouse and Goofy. People are starting to look at him funny. So, I shake him to wake him up.

"Oi Mick wake up."

Nope that is not working, I grab my bottle of water and pour it over his face.

"Earth to Mick, are you in there?"

"What do you think you are doing? First, you drug me, now you are pouring water over me."

"Oh boohoo. First off, you drugged yourself, and second, I am stopping you from becoming dehydrated. Third, you have been laying here all day, and the staff are starting to give you funny looks, especially when you were calling out for Minnie Mouse."

The staff bring our pizzas over and place them beside us.

"Here eat this," I say.

We eat our pizzas and he skulls some water.

"I am going to our room for a lay down," Mick says.

"Fair enough. Probably a good idea. You will get sun burnt if you keep laying out here."

Mick walks off to the room and I call up my friend Tinka who runs the orphanage I helped start and invite him over to the hotel for lunch and a swim.

"Hey Tinka, how is it all going?"

"Yes, all good Mr Jarrod. We had another two boys join us this week. They were living in a shanty under a bridge. So, now we have twenty-eight kids in total living in the house."

"Awesome stuff."

We have lunch and talk about plans for another house to be built on the land I recently purchased in May. By purchase I mean I gave the money to Tinka to purchase it under his name. As an Australian, I can own the building but not the land, but Tinka being Thai can own it. So, as long as Tinka does not screw me over, it will be all good. I met him when I was volunteering with that church, and I believe he is in this for the right reasons. If not, he is a very good actor. We also talk about getting a full-time teacher in there to teach English and Maths. I love knowing that one person can make a difference to many.

Who knows, I could have been me born into their life and they could have been born into mine.

My end goal is to have at least eight houses all up and running and self-sustaining before I die.

I say bye to Tinka and head up to the room to check on Mick. I walk into the room, and he is still sleeping.

"Get up," I say, shaking him. "It's seven o'clock. You have slept the whole day. Let's go have some fun."

"Sounds good."

We have showers and get changed. Then we head out to one of the many bars that line the streets.

"Hey, does she look familiar?" I ask while pointing out a familiar Thai girl.

Mick looks over and sees it is Joy. The bar girl Bob is in love with, and she is arm in arm with some other short fat guy in his mid-fifties.

"Well, at least she has a type. He could be Bob's twin," Mick says.

"Yep, and any bet that sucker is sending her money over each month as well."

I take my phone out and snap a pic of Joy and Bob's twin. "Might as well break his heart sooner rather than later and it will save him money in the long run."

I take a couple of photos of me with the couple in the background just in case I want to send a funny I told you so pic to Bob. Ha ha. That would be funny.

We go from one bar to the next, using up their happy hour deals. Suddenly a local guy jumps out of nowhere.

"You want to see ping pong show?" He asks.

"No thanks," Mick answers.

"Yes. He does. Let's go," I say. God, you cannot come all the way to Thailand and not watch a ping pong show. These girls go to great lengths to learn these tricks.

We enter an arena like the Muay Thai one. On the stage are the ladies doing their thing. There is a real mixture of people in the crowd. A married couple, a group of girls that look like they are on a hen's night, some Japanese tourists and us. The hen's night girls are having a great time, and one catches the ping-pong ball.

Next, a lady from the stage brings out a balloon and hands it to the married couple, who are told to hold it up high above their heads. The girl on the stage props up her legs and shoots out a little dart, popping the balloon.

"Wow! She has a good aim," Mick says.

"Yeah. I am sure she has had plenty of practice."

We stay for another twenty minutes, then decide to hit a couple more bars.

"Pretty talented girls," Mick says.

"Yeah. They are."

"The people watching are not as seedy as I thought they would be."

"Yeah. I guess everyone hears about these shows and wants to know for themselves what all the fuss is about."

"Yeah. Sounds about right."

We do lots of shots at the next bar and are getting hammered. We eventually end up at a lady boy bar and play pool with them. I know you might think I hate lady boys after the Jackie thing and the, my first head job story that I told you but as long as they are not trying to have sex with me it is all good.

One of the lady boys brings out some ecstasy pills and Mick and I have one each. It is a great night and I end up dancing on the bar with one of the lady boys named Rose. Since I am on ecstasy I am in a very loving mood and I am even dirty dancing with Rose, it is harmless fun and Mick is dancing with Rose's friend Nadia and what the fuck? Mick is making out with her. I take a photo to show him tomorrow. He probably won't even remember it. I have a couple more shots and dance a bit more and then I realise I cannot see Mick. I ask Rose.

"Hey Rose, have you seen my friend?"

"He in boom boom room."

"Boom boom room. What the fuck?"

"Yes, you can watch if you want?"

"What? What do you mean watch?"

"Come with me."

Rose leads me into a room with a big glass window and there on the other side of the window in Mick having sex with Nadia.

"What the fuck?"

I did not take a photo of this. I think no way will he want a photo of that getting out. I remember back to when Uncle Jeff had taken the hidden camera footage of me getting a head job off that lady boy and how fucked up that was. So, I take out my phone and delete the photo of Mick kissing Nadia. Poor Mick does not have to go through what I went through. He looks like he is having fun, so I just leave him to it.

"You want another pill?" Rose asks me.

"Yeah, why not."

We pop a pill and have a shot of sambuca. Then I see Mick walking out of the boom boom room and up to the bar.

"Hey Tim, I am having the best night of my life," Mick says with the biggest smile on his face. "I love you man. Thanks for bringing me to Thailand, you are my best friend. Also, I don't care about Bec cheating on me. That bitch. I mean I should not call her a bitch. She is a blessing in disguise. If she did not cheat on me, then I would not have come to Thailand with you and I would not be having the best night of my life. Do you want to know something Tim?"

"Ha ha. Yeah, what Mick?"

"I love you. I mean I really love you. Not in a gay way but in, you know like in a way like you are my brother and best friend and everything. Am I making sense?"

Wow! Mick is off his head. I must admit I am pretty fucked, and I can feel this second pill starting to kick in. I think it might be time to make our way back to our hotel.

"Yes, you are making perfect sense Mick. Hey, do you want to go back to the hotel? I think it would be a good idea."

"You know what I think we should do? We should go back to the hotel I think that would be a good idea."

"Ha ha, me too Mick. Great idea. Ha ha."

"What hotel are you staying at?" Rose asks.

"Ramada Thailand."

"I will walk you back."

"Okay."

"Just pay your bill."

"Okay."

And off we go walking back to our hotel.

We get back to our room and raid the mini bar. Drinking all the little bottles of spirts and eating all the overpriced snacks. Rose cranks up some music on her phone. It is heaps of fun. Mick keeps telling me and Rose that he loves us and that he is having the time of his life and how he is in love with Sofia and that he will marry her. That she is the love of his life. Mick eventually lays down on his bed and passes out.

I lay on my bed with Rose, and we start making out and we have sex. I wake up an hour or so later to hear Mick throwing up. I get a flash back of that ACDC singer dying from chocking on his own spew and I quickly get out of bed and roll him onto his side and tilt his head back to keep his airway open.

With Mick all good I go back to bed.

I wake up in the morning with a throbbing headache and sore teeth. I always grind my teeth when I am on ecstasy.

"Good morning, big boy."

Oh yeah, I get a flash back to last night and try to remember as much as I can.

"Good morning," I say back.

What is her name again? Oh yeah it is Rose, and she is not actually a girl. But honestly, you know what? She was really cool last night. I guess it does not really matter if you are a guy or a girl or a cross between the two. I reckon you just have to go with the person's personality.

"My name is Rose. Did you forget?"

"Honestly, I did for a second, but I remember now. Do you remember my name?"

"Yes, Jarrod but your friend calls you Tim."

"Yep, that is right."

"I am going to have a shower now."

"Okay."

I lay there relaxing, and I think of Jackie. Maybe I judged her too quickly. I did think she was a pretty cool chick before I found out about her dick. I think I will apologise and see if she wants to give it a go.

Rose comes out of the shower.

"Do you want me to stay or go?"

"Umm. Is it cool if you go?"

"No problem. You pay me for last night 3000 baht."

I was just about to haggle over the price with her but, it was a great night, and I did have a big awakening that might change my life forever. So, 3000 baht is fine.

"No worries. I will grab you some cash."

I go to my wallet, and it is empty. I am not surprised we drunk a fair bit of piss last night, plus the pills. I pressed my pin number into the hotel safe and give her a hundred dollars Australian.

"Thanks. Will you come to the bar again tonight?'

"Maybe, maybe not."

"Ok, no problem. Have a fun holiday."

And with that, she leaves my room.

I have a shower and chuck on my board shorts and a t-shirt. I am starving. I don't know what the time is, but I am pretty sure I have missed breakfast. I walk down to the pool to look for Mick.

There he is in the pool next to the swim up bar having a beer just like yesterday. I sneak up to him and do a big bommie right next to him splashing water over him and his beer.

"Oi," says the barman.

"Sorry mate. Yeah, that was a bit stupid. Hey, can I please order a Singha beer and a big tropical burger."

"Yes sir."

"Hey Mick, what a night?" I say.

"Yeah, where is the girl?" Mick asks.

"Oh her. She is gone. I cannot wait for this burger I am starving."

I wonder if he remembers having sex with that ladyboy. Hmm, I will just ask and judge his reaction. He might not want to talk about it. I don't really want to talk about mine if he does not remember or want to talk about his.

"Did you have fun last night?" I ask.

"Yeah, it was good from what I can remember. How did we get home?"

"We walked."

"Oh, okay."

"What was the last thing you remember?"

"I remember us hitting up lots of bars and the last thing I remember is playing pool with some locals and the next thing I know I am waking up with spew all over myself."

"Yeah, you actually woke me up and I rolled you onto your side, so you did not die in your sleep. Basically, I saved your life. Ha ha."

"Well thank you."

"Do you remember taking ecstasy?"

"What? Really? Na, I don't remember that. Are you messing with me?"

"Nope."

"Oh shit. Well, that would be the first time I have taken ecstasy and I don't even remember it. Ha ha."

Classic. Well, it looks like he does not remember anything about him and that lady boy and by him asking where that girl is, he must think she is a real girl. So, no harm no foul. Time to drop the subject.

"You want to go jet-skiing and parasailing today," I ask.

"Hell yeah, bring it on."

"If it is okay with you, I might just give the bars a miss for the rest of the trip. We can do some tours, and you can shop until you drop if you want? Ha ha."

"Ha ha. Sounds good to me."

The rest of the trip is great. We hire jet skis, do a boat tour to some islands, white water rafting, and Mick buys heaps of fake brand label clothes. He even gets good at bartering.

Fly out day. Well fly back to Perth day. I am relaxing on the plane watching a movie when Mick turns to me.

"Hey, did you have sex with that Thai chick?"

"Yeah, of course I did. But do not tell Jackie. I think I am going to apologise to her and see what happens there. Why are you asking me that?"

"No reason. I was just wondering."

"Oh, okay."

We sit back, put our headphones back on and watch our movies. Why would he ask me that? Does he know she was a he? I wonder if he is starting to remember what happened that night.

"Hey, do you remember getting laid that night we went out on the piss?"

"No I didn't"

"Ha ha. Yes, you did."

"No, I didn't. Did I?"

"Yep."

"Was she hot."

"Yeah, I guess so. She was not ugly. I guess she was good for her age."

"What? How old was she?"

"I would guess mid-sixties."

"Fuck off. You're making this shit up."

"Yeah, I am. She was definitely mid-seventies."

"You are such a dick."

"Na, I am just fucking with you. You didn't get laid."

"Oh good, I would like to remember it if I did. Otherwise, what's the point?"

We sit back again and watch our movies.

I get back to work and apologise to Jackie and I eventually open-up to her and tell her what happened to me when I was younger and that was the reason, I acted the way I did. She is cool about it, and it feels good telling someone about it. It is a freeing experience. I did not realise the weight I had been carrying all these years.

A year later and we are all at the wet mess on shift change. Mick, George, Johnno, Sofia, Jackie and I are all having drinks together. I go up to the bar and order us a round of drinks. I come back to the table.

"Here you go guys," as I pass out the drinks.

"Cheers Tim," they all say.

I get to Jackie, I put her drink down in front of her and then I go down on one knee.

"Jackie Earl Thomson, will you marry me?" I ask.

"Oh my god. Yes Jarrod, of course I will."

"Fuck yeah."

"Whoop whoop! Congrats guys," George says.

"Congratulations," they all say.

"Cheers to Tim and Jackie," says Johnno and we all take a drink.

How awesome, she said yes. I am so happy.

Alright reader this is where you have a choice. The book has turned into one of those choose you own adventure books. You know, like the ones we used to have as kids.

So, here is your choice, you can stop reading now and the book finishes on a happy note the same as the last two books where the guy gets the girl and lives happily ever after, or you keep reading and things get messed up.

To all those who are choosing the happy ending, I just want to say a big thanks for buying the book, there will be more of these FIFO books to come. Have a fantastic day.

Alright, now we have all the softies gone let's get into it.

The next 6 months is good. I get a promotion to supervisor and Jackie moves into my place. Unfortunately, there is a bit of a downturn in the mining industry and the company we work for are forced to lay off quite a few workers. I keep my job, but Jackie loses hers and cannot get another one straight away. She tells me she is applying for roles but just cannot get one. So, for the next couple of months I work my two and one and she just hangs around the house. She is catching up with some of her old friends who I do not like, they are losers, and she is starting to go out a lot more.

One night on night shift Jackie calls me.

"Hey Jackie, what's up?"

"Where are you?" Jackie asks in an accusatory tone.

"Where do you think? I am at work."

"Oh yeah. Who are you with?"

"I am in a light vehicle. By myself. What's with the tone?"

"Is Emily with you?"

"Excuse me?"

"You heard me."

"No, Emily is not with me. She is in a truck, working. Why the hell would Emily be with me?"

"I know you are fucking her."

"What the fuck? Are you drunk?"

"I have had a couple but that is beside the point. Why are you cheating on me?"

"I am not bloody cheating on you."

"I know you are. Am I not enough for you? You said you love me and now you pull this shit. You are such an asshole."

And with that she hangs up. I try calling her back a couple of times to no avail. I hope she just drinks some water and sleeps it off.

Obviously, this no working is getting to her, the poor bugger has already spent all her savings and I am having to pay all the bills and give her spending money. Well really, she pays the bills but with my money, I figure if she is at least in charge of the budget it will give her some purpose. You can go insane from boredom if you have literally nothing to do and you can only watch so much Netflix and judging by that last phone call that is exactly what is slowly happening to her. Maybe I should suggest to her to get a hobby?

Ring ring. My phone springs to life. I look at the caller id and it is my mum. What the hell? It is 10pm at night, she should be asleep.

"Hello," I answer.

"Jarrod, sorry to call you so late," Mum replies.

"All good. I am on night shift. I will be awake all night. What's up?"

"Jackie called me in hysterics. She told be you are cheating on her with a girl named Emily."

"Oh my god. No, I am not cheating on Jackie and if you knew what Emily looks like, trust me, I can get someone a lot better looking than her to cheat on Jackie with."

"So, what's going on? Why is Jackie thinking you are?"

"She called me earlier and she admitted she had been drinking. I think all this not working is doing her head in."

"Have you tried calling her to straighten it out?"

"Yep, but she is not answering her phone. Don't worry about it Mum, go back to sleep."

"Okay Jarrod, if there is anything I can do just let me know."

"Thanks Mum. Night."

That's the problem with working up North, you cannot just nip a problem in the butt, face to face. Unless of course you tell your supervisor, it is an emergency and then you will have to catch a plane back home which will probably take a day or two to organise the flight.

I flick her a text saying I am not cheating, and I think she should take up a hobby and I would pay for it. I get nothing back.

The next day I get a call from Jackie.

"Hey, how are you going? How was your night?"

"Fine until you called?"

"I didn't call you last night."

"Yes, you did, and you also called my Mum, telling her I was cheating on you with Emily."

"What? I don't remember any of that."

"How much did you drink last night?"

"I had a couple, but I was probably overtired on top of that. I haven't been sleeping well lately."

"Have you tried sleeping pills or that melatonin stuff?"

"Na, I will get some."

"I think you need a hobby. Just pick something and take the money out of the account."

"Thanks, that's probably a good idea, until I can get some work."

"Good stuff. Well, I had better get ready for work. Love you."

"Love you too."

Over the next week I had several strange text messages at random hours, accusing me of cheating and that someone was trying to break into the house.

Ring ring. I call Jackie.

"Hey Jackie, what's going on."

"The police have just left."

"Did they catch anyone?"

"They said they could not find any trace of anyone having been around the house, but I know someone was trying to break in I could hear them."

"Can you get someone to stay with you tonight? I will be home tomorrow, and I will organise an alarm system."

"Yeah, I have Sofia coming over soon."

"Alright, have every light on in the house until she comes over, just to scare anyone away."

"Will do."

"Alright see you tomorrow."

I fly home the next day and when I get home the front door is wide open.

"Hello, hey Jackie are you home?" I say as I walk in.

I check our bedroom which is the first room on the left as you walk into our house. Nope not there. I walk into the kitchen, and I see Jackie laying on the couch asleep.

I sneak up to her to give her a kiss on the cheek and WTF? There is a belt around her arm, a burnt spoon on the floor with a lighter and a syringe.

"Jackie, Jackie," I shout, shaking her. But she doesn't come too. "Shit, shit."

I grab my phone and call 000.

"Police, fire or ambulance?" The operator asks.

"Ambulance." I yell, waiting what feels like ages until I get through.

Finally, a female voice answers. "Ambulance. What's the address of the emergency there?"

"It's my fiancé, she's..."

"I need your exact address so we can get paramedics on their way to you while you give me the rest of the details"

"It's 34 Bluestone Way, Bertram."

"Thank you, now tell me exactly what's happened."

"It's my fiancé, she has shot something up and od'd."

"How old is your fiancé?"

"27."

"And is she awake?"

"No, she's not."

"Is she breathing?"

"Umm I will check."

I put my cheek next to her mouth and I cannot feel anything.

"No, she is not."

"Do you know how to do CPR?"

"Yes."

"Now, place her on her back and I'll talk you through it."

I press the speaker button and place the phone on the ground next to Jackie and I start compressions. Listening to the call taker's instructions and answering more questions.

"I'm going to stay on the line with you until the paramedics arrive. You're doing great"

"Ok."

I can hear sirens nearby and keep pressing on her chest while the voice on the phone counts with me until I hear a knock at the door before it opens.

"Hello, ambulance."

"Yeah, in here," I yell back.

"It's alright, we'll take it from here. You've done a great job," says one of the paramedics.

One of them takes over with compressions while the other sticks defibrillator pads on Jackie's chest and hits the button on the monitor nearby.

"Off the chest." And they pause, hands hovering over her for a second while the machine does its thing. "Stand clear." As the defibrillator shocks Jackie, her chest thrusts upwards before settling back on the floor and they kick back into action.

"Clear." I hear them call at the same time as another couple of green uniforms arrive and take over with compressions. Someone hands me a piece of paper to fill in, they're asking questions, our names, what's happened, her medical history and more.

Opening bags now, unwrapping packages, connecting oxygen, fastening a tourniquet around her arm. Unable to look any longer, I stand with my back to the scene, listening to them try it time and time again. Repeating the cycle.

"Jarrod." One of them comes over and places a blue gloved hand on my back. "Jarrod. We're going to stop now. We've been pumping Jackie's heart and breathing for her for over forty minutes. There's nothing more we can do for her, she's dead."

"I want to see her." Everything is still now. The noise and movement have all stopped and I turn around to look.

"Of course. We need you not to touch anything, but you can sit down here. All we're going to do is take our equipment away, but we have to leave the breathing tube and everything else in place for now, okay?"

"What happens now?" I ask.

"Well, I'll stay with you here and my colleagues will pack things away and make a couple of phone calls. One of them will be to let the police know, that's perfectly normal whenever someone dies at home unexpectedly. So, we'll let them get on with all of that, do you have any questions, or want to just sit quietly here with me? We can go to another room or outside if you prefer?"

I sit in silence for a what feels like an eternality. People in uniforms come and collect her body and take her to the morgue. I call my mum to come over. I don't know who else to call.

Sofia was supposed to be with her. Why is she not here? I call Sofia.

"Hey Tim, what's up?" Sofia answers.

"Jackie's dead."

"What? I think I heard you wrong."

"I said Jackie is dead. She overdosed on something. Were you here last night?"

"No, we were at Mick's parents place and then we came home. Oh my god, I can't believe it."

"Jackie said you were coming over last night."

"No, I haven't spoken to Jackie since last week. Oh my god I, I."

She goes silent and then bursts out crying. I can hear Mick in the background trying to calm her down.

"Tim is that you?" Mick says into the phone.

"Yep. Hey Mick."

"What's going on? What did you say to Sofia she is crying, and she won't say why?"

"Jackie is dead Mick."

"What? Really? How?"

"She overdosed on drugs. I just got home, and she was dead on the couch."

"Oh, I am so sorry Tim. Do you want me to come over?"

"Na, it's alright. I have mum coming over. Hey was Sofia with you all night."

"Yeah, she was. Why?"

"All good. It's just Jackie said she was coming over last night."

"Na, she was definitely with me all night."

"Cheers Mick. I'll let you go."

"Sorry man. If you need anything just let me know. Okay."

"Yeah, thanks."

I hang up and think to myself.

"Who did Jackie get the drugs off? And was anyone else with her or did she do this by herself. Is this my fault? Should I have come home sooner or done something differently, do I call her parents or were the cops supposed to do that? I can't remember if they told me if they were going to do it."

I have so many questions but I, I…

Knock knock.

Who could that be?

The end...

I know, you are thinking excuse me. Who is at the door? Well, I will tell you in the next book. Ha ha (evil laugh).

And there you have it ladies and gentlemen. I hope you enjoyed the book. Let me know what you think on my social media and tell all your friends to buy a copy. Have a fantastic day and see you soon in FIFO 4. Aaron.

About the Author

Aaron started his mining career as a driller's offsider, on an RC drill rig, back in 2003. Then he landed a job doing FIFO, as a blast crew labourer and earnt his shot firers licence. When he realised a dump truck operator got paid the same as a shotfirer, he made the transition into the air conditioning and has been operating the big mining machines ever since.

He has self-published eight children's books and is currently writing this FIFO series.